★

US MILITARY BRANCHES

THE US COAST GUARD IN ACTION

Marie-Therese Miller

Lerner Publications ◆ Minneapolis

Handwritten: To James, Andrew & Gregory, Cheers to the Coast Guard!

Handwritten: Love Marie-Therese Miller

To John, Harold, Warren, and to all my family members and friends
who have served in the US military
With heartfelt gratitude to Coast Guard personnel

Lerner Publications Company
An imprint of Lerner Publishing Group, Inc.
241 First Avenue North
Minneapolis, MN 55401 USA

For reading levels and more information, look up this title at www.lernerbooks.com.

Main body text set in ITC Franklin Gothic Std.
Typeface provided by Adobe Systems.

Designer: Mary Ross

Library of Congress Cataloging-in-Publication Data

Names: Miller, Marie-Therese, author.
Title: The US Coast Guard in action / Marie-Therese Miller.
Description: Minneapolis: Lerner Publications, [2023] | Series: US military
    branches (Updog books) | Includes bibliographical references and index. |
    Audience: Ages 8–11 | Audience: Grades 4–6 | Summary: "For hundreds of
    years, the Coast Guard has protected the US's waterways. Discover the Coast
    Guard's ships, rescue missions, and more!"—Provided by publisher.
Identifiers: LCCN 2021045370 (print) | LCCN 2021045371 (ebook) |
    ISBN 9781728458298 (library binding) | ISBN 9781728463605 (paperback) |
    ISBN 9781728462509 (ebook)
Subjects: LCSH: United States. Coast Guard—Juvenile literature.
Classification: LCC VG53 .M55 2023 (print) | LCC VG53 (ebook) |
    DDC 363.28/60973—dc23

LC record available at https://lccn.loc.gov/2021045370
LC ebook record available at https://lccn.loc.gov/2021045371

Manufactured in the United States of America
1-50858-50195-2/1/2022

TABLE OF CONTENTS

ALWAYS READY

A man sailing on the ocean gets caught in a terrible storm.

The US Coast Guard battles the storm and rescues him.

The Coast Guard
was formed in 1790.

UNITED STATES
REVENUE CUTTER

It patrols the oceans and other waterways to protect the US.

WATERWAY:
river, canal, or other body of water that boats travel

UP NEXT!

MANY MISSIONS

Search and rescue is one of the Coast Guard's many missions.

MISSION:
an important job or task

The Coast Guard also helps during natural disasters.

It keeps US waters safe from pollution, such as oil spills.

The Coast Guard places and fixes buoys. It also takes care of lighthouses so ships can travel safely.

BUOY:
a floating marker that shows boats where to go

VEHICLE CLOSE-UP

The USCGC *Healy* is the Coast Guard's largest polar icebreaker at 420 feet (128 m) long.

main mast

radio antenna

main deck

U. S. COAST GUARD

20

science lab

UP NEXT!
Coast Guard vehicles.

SHIPS, BOATS, AND AIRCRAFT

Icebreakers cut through thick, polar ice.

These ships are used to get researchers and supplies to the Arctic and Antarctica.

Coast Guard boats are smaller than 65 feet (20 m).

The 47-foot (14 m) motor lifeboat is quick and perfect for rescues.

A rescue swimmer can jump from a Jayhawk helicopter into the water to save someone.

Then the person is hoisted onto the Jayhawk using a basket.

The Coast Guard has about forty-eight thousand members who protect the US and its waterways.

MILITARY MISSION

SOMEONE FELL INTO THE OCEAN. WHAT SHOULD THE COAST GUARD USE TO RESCUE THEM?

A. The *Healy*

B. Buoy or lighthouse

C. Jayhawk helicopter

Answer: C

GLOSSARY

buoy: a floating marker that shows boats where to go

mission: an important job or task

waterway: river, canal, or other body of water that boats travel

CHECK IT OUT!

Ducksters: United States Armed Forces
https://www.ducksters.com/history/us_government/united
_states_armed_forces.php

Kiddle: United States Coast Guard Facts for Kids
https://kids.kiddle.co/United_States_Coast_Guard

London, Martha. *US Coast Guard Equipment and Vehicles*.
Minneapolis: Abdo, 2022.

Military Kids Connect: Military Life
https://militarykidsconnect.health.mil/Military-Life

Miller, Marie-Therese. *The US Navy in Action*. Minneapolis: Lerner
Publications, 2023.

Morey, Allan. *U.S. Coast Guard*. Minneapolis: Pogo Books, 2021.

INDEX

PHOTO ACKNOWLEDGMENTS

Image credits: Navy Petty Officer 3rd Class Ryan Dickinson/United States Department of Defense, Cover; U.S. Coast Guard, pp. 3, 5, 6, 7, 8, 9, 11, 12–13, 14, 15, 16, 17, 18, 19, 20; Konstantin Tkach/Shutterstock.com, p. 4; FashionStock.com/Shutterstock.com, p. 10.

Cover image: Navy Petty Officer 3rd Class Ryan Dickinson/United States Department of Defense.